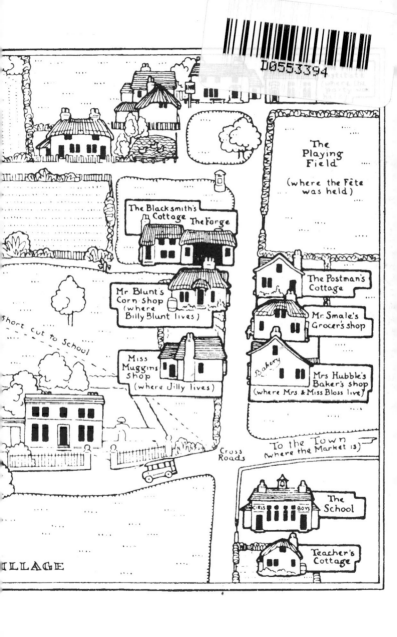

MILLY-MOLLY-MOLLY-MANDY'S

Summer

Milly-Molly-Mandy books

Adventures
Family
Friends
School Days

Spring
Summer
Autumn
Winter

Joyce Lankester Brisley

MILLY-MOLLY-MANDY'S

Summer

MACMILLAN CHILDREN'S BOOKS

The stories in this collection first appeared in
Further Doings of Milly-Molly-Mandy (1932)
Milly-Molly-Mandy Again (1948)
Milly-Molly-Mandy and Billy Blunt (1967)
Milly-Molly-Mandy & Co. (1955)
More of Milly-Molly-Mandy (1929)
Published by George G. Harrap & Co. Ltd

This edition published 2012 by Macmillan Children's Books
a division of Macmillan Publishers Limited
20 New Wharf Road, London N1 9RR
Basingstoke and Oxford
Associated companies throughout the world
www.panmacmillan.com

ISBN 978-1-4472-0800-6

1 3 5 7 9 8 6 4 2

A CIP catalogue record for this book is available from the British Library.

Printed and bound in China

Publisher's Note
*The stories in this collection are reproduced in the form in which they appeared
upon first publication in the UK by George G. Harrap & Co. Ltd.
All spellings remain consistent with these original editions.*

Contents

The Nice White Cottage with the Thatched Roof (where Milly-Molly-Mandy lives)

Brook

The Meadow (where M·M·M and Billy Blunt practised racing)

The Barn (where M·M·M gave a party)

The Moggs's Cottage (where little-friend-Susan lives)

Short cut to school (only used in dry weather)

Woods

To Another Village

MAP of the

Joyce Lankester Brisley

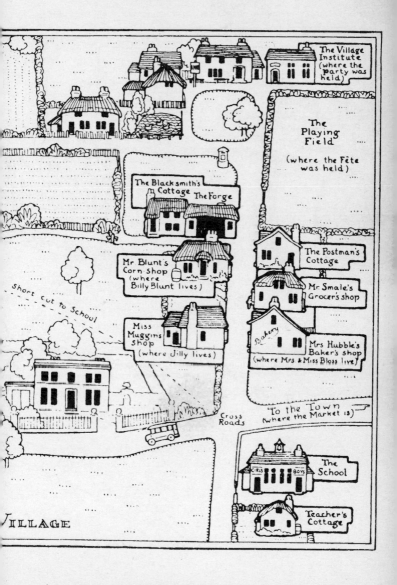

Milly-Molly-Mandy Gets Up Early

Once upon a time, one beautiful summer morning, Milly-Molly-Mandy woke up very early.

She knew it was very early, because Father and Mother were not moving (Milly-Molly-Mandy's cot-bed was in one corner of Father's and Mother's room). And she knew it was a beautiful summer morning, because the cracks around the window-blinds were so bright she could hardly look at them.

Milly-Molly-Mandy (whose full name was really Millicent Margaret Amanda) knelt up on the foot of her cot-bed and softly lifted one corner of the blind, and peeped out.

And it was the most beautiful, quiet summer morning that ever was.

The doves in the dove-cote were saying "*Coo-roo-o-o!*" to each other, in a soft, lazy sort of way; and the hens round the hen-house in the field were saying "*Ker-ruk-ruk!*" to each other, in a soft, busy sort of way; and Old Marmaduke the cock was yelling "*Doodle-doo!*" to everybody, at the top of his voice, only it sounded soft because he was right the other side of the barn.

"Well!" said Milly-Molly-Mandy to herself. "It's much too beautiful a morning to stay in bed till breakfast-time. I think I'll get up very, very quietly, so's not to wake Father and Mother."

So Milly-Molly-Mandy slid out of bed

very, very quietly, and she slid into her socks, and into her clothes as far as her petticoat.

And then she crept to the wash-stand, but she didn't think she could manage the big water-jug without waking Father and Mother. So she took up her shoes and her pink-striped cotton frock, and she creepy-crept to the door and opened it, only making just one tiny little click.

And then she creepy-crept down the stairs, without disturbing Grandpa or Grandma or Uncle or Aunty, into the kitchen.

It looked funny and dark in the kitchen, for the curtains were still drawn. Topsy the cat jumped off Grandma's chair and came yawning and stretching to meet her, and

Milly-Molly-Mandy had to stoop down and let Topsy the cat dab her little cold nose very, very lightly against her warm cheek, for "Good morning".

And then Milly-Molly-Mandy went into the scullery to wash.

But when she turned on the tap she suddenly thought of the brook at the bottom of the meadow. So she just washed her hands and neck and saved her face to wash in the brook. And then she put on her frock and shoes and softly unlocked the back door, and slipped outside.

It really was a most beautiful fresh morning, full of little bird-voices; and Toby the dog was making little thumping noises in his kennel, because he had heard her and was excited to think somebody was up.

So Milly-Molly-Mandy ran and let him off the chain, but she held his collar and whispered, "Hush, Toby! Hush, Toby!" very sternly, until they got as far as the meadow.

Then she let him go, and Toby the dog barked and capered, and Milly-Molly-Mandy, with the breeze in her hair, ran hoppity-skip down to the brook through the long grass and dewdrops that sparkled all colours in the sun.

The water looked so lovely and clear and cold, rippling over the stones, that Milly-Molly-Mandy couldn't decide all at once which was the nicest spot to wash her face in. So she was walking along beside it a little way, when suddenly whom should she see in the next field but little-friend-Susan, up early too.

"Su-san!" called Milly-Molly-Mandy.

"Milly-Molly-Mandy!" called little-friend-Susan. "There're mushrooms in this field!"

So Milly-Molly-Mandy and Toby the dog ran and clambered through the railings into the next field. And there *were* mushrooms in that field, for Milly-Molly-Mandy nearly trod on one straight away. Only she just didn't – she picked it and ran to show it to little-friend-Susan and say, "Fancy you being up so early, Susan!" And little-friend-Susan ran to show Milly-Molly-Mandy her three mushrooms and say, "Fancy you being up so early, Milly-Molly-Mandy!"

Then they searched all over the field together, but they didn't find any more mushrooms. And then they came to another field, and suddenly whom should they see in the middle of the other field but Billy Blunt, up early too.

"Bil-ly!" called Milly-Molly-Mandy.

"Mushrooms!" called Billy Blunt.

So Milly-Molly-Mandy and little-

"There're mushrooms in this field!"

friend-Susan and Toby the dog ran and clambered over the stile into the other field, and went to show Billy Blunt their mushrooms and say, "Fancy you being up so early, Billy!" And Billy Blunt came to show them his two mushrooms and say, "Fancy anybody stopping in bed!"

And then they found quite a lot of mushrooms growing together in one patch, and they all gave a gasp and a shout and set to work picking in great excitement.

When they had finished gathering whom should they see coming into the field with a basket over his arm but a shabby boy who had run in a race with Billy Blunt at a fête last Bank Holiday (and beaten him!).

He seemed to be looking for mushrooms too; and as he came near Milly-Molly-Mandy smiled at him a bit, and he smiled a bit back. And little-friend-Susan said, "Hullo!" and he said, "Hullo!" And Billy

Blunt said, "Plenty of mushrooms here."
And the boy said, "Are there?"

Then Milly-Molly-Mandy said, "Look what we've got!" And the boy looked.

And then little-friend-Susan said, "How many've you got?" And the boy showed his basket, but there weren't many in it.

And then Billy Blunt said, "What are you going to do with them?"

And the boy said, "Sell them to Mr Smale the Grocer, if I can get enough. If not, we eat them, my grandad and I. Only we'd rather have the money."

Then Milly-Molly-Mandy said, "Let's help to get the basket full!"

So they spread about over the field and looked everywhere for mushrooms, and they really got quite a lot; but the basket wasn't full. Then Billy Blunt and Milly-Molly-Mandy and little-friend-Susan looked questioningly at each other and at their own heap of mushrooms, and then they nodded to each other and piled them all into the basket.

"My word!" said the boy, with a beaming face. "Won't Grandad be pleased today!" Then he thanked them all very much and said good-bye and went off home.

Milly-Molly-Mandy and little-friend-Susan and Billy Blunt felt very satisfied with their morning's work. They had enjoyed it so much that they made plans to get up early another morning and go mushrooming together, with baskets –

for themselves, this time.

And then they all said "Good-bye" till they should meet again for school, and Milly-Molly-Mandy called Toby the dog, and they went off home to their breakfast.

And it wasn't until she got in that Milly-Molly-Mandy remembered she had never washed her face in the brook after all, and she had to go up and do it in a basin in the ordinary way!

Milly-Molly-Mandy Makes a Garden

Once upon a time Milly-Molly-Mandy was very excited.

There was to be a grand Flower and Vegetable Show in the village in a month's time (the posters telling about it were stuck on the back of the forge); and besides prizes being given for all the usual things – such as the finest potatoes and strawberries and garden flowers, and the best home-made jams and pickles – there were also to be prizes for the prettiest posy of wild flowers, and the best miniature garden (grown in a bowl).

"Ooh!" said Milly-Molly-Mandy to little-friend-Susan (they were reading the poster together after morning school); "I wonder!"

"What!" said little-friend-Susan.

"I wonder," said Milly-Molly-Mandy, "if I shall grow a little garden in a bowl, and send it to the Flower Show!"

"Oh, could you?" said little-friend-Susan. "And do you suppose I could make a posy and send it in too? Wouldn't it be lovely to win a prize?"

"I don't suppose we could," said Milly-Molly-Mandy, "but it would be such fun to try. I'm going to ask Mother."

So when Milly-Molly-Mandy got home she asked if she might make a little garden and send it to the Flower Show. And Mother said, "If you can make it nicely enough you may, Milly-Molly-Mandy. Father is going to send in some of his best

gooseberries, and I am going to send some pots of jam and pickles; so we shall make a good showing, all together!"

Then Mother got out a brown pottery pie-dish from the kitchen cupboard and asked Milly-Molly-Mandy if she thought that would do to grow her garden in; and after Milly-Molly-Mandy had considered it well she thought it would. She put some broken bits of flower pot at the bottom (to help to drain off the wet), and then she filled the dish with the brownest, softest earth she could find. And then she had to think what to plant in her garden so that it would look just like a real big one, if it weren't so very little!

It took a lot of thinking.

After school Milly-Molly-Mandy told Billy Blunt about the Flower Show in case he hadn't about it; but he said he had.

"Are you going to go in for any of the prizes?" asked Milly-Molly-Mandy.

"Huh!" was all Billy Blunt said; but Milly-Molly-Mandy knew he was!

"Which one?" she asked. And Billy Blunt took her into the old cycle-shed beside the corn-shop and showed her – a fine new red earthenware bowl filled with soft brown earth!

Showed her a fine new red earthenware bowl

"Billy!" said Milly-Molly-Mandy. "Fancy your going in for that one! So am I! And we can't both win the prize."

"Don't suppose either of us will," said Billy Blunt, "but I mean to have a good try."

"So do I," said Milly-Molly-Mandy.

"And the best one wins," said Billy Blunt.

The next day Milly-Molly-Mandy set the first plant in her garden. It was a tiny little holly-tree which she had found growing almost in the path under the big holly-tree by the hedge. (It had grown from one of the fallen berries.) Milly-Molly-Mandy knew it would only be trodden on if left there, so she carefully dug it up and planted it in the soft brown earth in her bowl.

Next she went poking about down by the brook, and she found some nice moss-grown bits of rotten wood; one bit looked just like a little green mossy cave, so she took it home and put it in the bowl by the holly-tree; and then she planted some grass and a daisy root in the rest of the space, and it really looked quite a pretty garden. It grew so nicely, and the baby holly-tree opened out its new little leaves as if it felt quite at home there.

Billy Blunt wouldn't let anyone see his garden until he had got it arranged to his liking. And then one day he said Milly-Molly-Mandy might have a look if she liked. And he fetched it down from his bedroom to show her.

And it was pretty!

There was more room in Billy Blunt's bowl, and he had made it like a rock garden with rough-looking little stones; and a small sycamore-tree was growing between them in one place, and a wee sage-bush in another; and little tiny plants – scarlet pimpernels, and rock-roses, and lady's bedstraw – sprouted here and there. Milly-Molly-Mandy did like it.

"Oh, Billy!" she said, "yours is much prettier than mine! Except that yours hasn't got a cave in it. You'll get the prize."

But when Billy Blunt saw the mossy cave in Milly-Molly-Mandy's garden he wasn't so sure.

The day of the Flower Show drew near. It was to be held in the village Institute on the Saturday, and everybody who was going to send in (and nearly everybody was) was feeling very busy and important. Mr Jakes the Postman had some fine gooseberries and red-currants which he meant to enter, and little-friend-Susan said her father and Mrs Green were going to show lots of flowers and vegetables from the garden at the Big House with the iron railings (Mr Moggs was gardener at Mrs Green's), and Mrs Green was making a miniature garden too.

And then, just the very day before the Show (which, of course, was sending-in day), what DO you think happened?

Billy Blunt's little sycamore-tree lost all its leaves!

Either he hadn't managed to get all its roots when he dug it up or else it had been left too long in the hot sun, without much earth to grow in; anyhow, when he came back from school there it was, with its leaves all curled up and spoiled.

Billy Blunt was dreadfully disappointed, and so was Milly-Molly-Mandy.

"Whole thing's done for now," said Billy Blunt; "it's nothing without that tree."

"Can't we find another one somewhere?" said Milly-Molly-Mandy. "Let's look!"

"I looked everywhere before I found that one," said Billy Blunt. "Besides, there isn't any time to look. It's got to go in. Only it's no good sending it now."

"Oh, Billy!" said Milly-Molly-Mandy. She was as disappointed as he was. "It won't be any fun sending mine in now. It wouldn't seem fair if I *did* get a prize. But I don't expect I'll get one anyhow – Susan says Mrs Green is sending in a garden."

"Hers won't have a cave in it," said Billy Blunt.

And then, suddenly, Milly-Molly-Mandy had an idea.

"I tell you what! Couldn't we make one

beautiful garden between us and send it in together? Why not? Your big bowl and garden, with my tree and the mossy cave? Couldn't we?"

Billy Blunt was very doubtful. "I don't know that we could send in together," he said slowly.

"Why couldn't we? Mr Moggs and Mrs Green at the Big House do," said Milly-Molly-Mandy. "I'll go and fetch my garden and we'll see how it would look!"

So she ran all the way home to the nice white cottage with the thatched roof and fetched her little garden; and then she walked carefully with it all the way back. And what do you think she found Billy Blunt doing? He was writing a label to see how it would look for the Flower Show: "Sent in by Billy Blunt and Milly-Molly-Mandy."

"Looks quite businesslike," he said. "Did you fetch your tree?"

The little garden in the pottery dish looked so pretty it almost seemed a pity to spoil it, but Milly-Molly-Mandy insisted. So together they took out the little holly-tree and planted it in place of the sycamore-tree; and then they arranged the mossy bit of wood at one side of the bowl; and it looked so real you almost felt as if you could live in the little green cave, and go clambering on the rocks, or climb the tree, if you wished!

"Well!" said Milly-Molly-Mandy, sitting back on her heels, "it just couldn't be prettier!"

"Umm!" said Billy Blunt, looking very satisfied. "It's prettier than either of them was before. Let's take it in now."

So they walked across to the Institute and handed in the precious miniature garden, with the sixpence entrance fee between them.

It was so hard to wait till the next day! But on Saturday, as soon as the judges had decided which things had won prizes, the Flower Show was opened and the shilling people could go in. Most people waited till the afternoon, when it cost only sixpence; Father and Mother and Grandpa and Grandma and Uncle and Aunty and Milly-Molly-Mandy (who was half-price) went then.

The place was filled with people and lovely smells of flowers and strawberries, and there was a great noise of people talking and exclaiming, and cups clattering somewhere at the back, and the village band was tuning up.

Milly-Molly-Mandy could not see Billy Blunt or the miniature gardens; but Father's gooseberries had got first prize, and his basket of vegetables second prize (Mr Moggs's got the first), and Mother had first prize for her jam, but nothing for her marrow-chutney (Mrs Critch, the Thatcher's wife, won that). Little-friend-Susan was there, skipping up and down gleefully because her wild posy had won a third prize.

And then Milly-Molly-Mandy saw Billy Blunt. He was grinning all over his face!

"Seen the gardens?" he said. "Come on. This way." And he pulled her through the crowd to a table at the farther end, where were arranged several miniature gardens of all sorts and sizes, some of them very pretty ones indeed.

But right in the middle, raised up by itself, was the prettiest one of all; and it was labelled:

"FIRST PRIZE. Sent in by Billy Blunt and Milly-Molly-Mandy"!

Milly-Molly-Mandy
Finds a Nest

Once upon a time, one warm summer morning, Uncle came quickly in at the back door of the nice white cottage with the thatched roof and shouted from the kitchen, "Milly-Molly-Mandy!"

Milly-Molly-Mandy, who was just coming downstairs carrying a big bundle of washing for Mother, called back, "Yes, Uncle?"

"Hi! quick!" said Uncle, and went outside the back door again.

Milly-Molly-Mandy couldn't think what Uncle wanted with her, but it had such an exciting sound she dropped the big bundle on the stairs in a hurry and ran down to the passage. But when she got to the passage she thought she ought not to leave the big bundle on the stairs, lest someone trip over it in the shadow; so she ran back again in a hurry and fetched the big bundle down, and ran along to the kitchen with it. But she was in such a hurry she dropped some things out of the big bundle and had to run back again and pick them up.

But at last she got them all on to the kitchen table, and then she ran out of the back door and said, "Yes, Uncle? What is it, Uncle?"

Uncle was just going through the

meadow gate, with some boards under one arm and the tool-box on the other. He beckoned to Milly-Molly-Mandy with his head (which was the only thing he had loose to do it with), so Milly-Molly-Mandy ran after him down the garden path to the meadow.

"Yes, Uncle?" said Milly-Molly-Mandy.

"Milly-Molly-Mandy," said Uncle, striding over the grass with his boards and tool-box, "I've found a nest."

"What sort of a nest?" said Milly-Molly-Mandy, hoppity-skipping a bit to keep up with him.

"Milly-Molly-Mandy," said Uncle, "I rather think it's a Milly-Molly-Mandy nest."

Milly-Molly-Mandy stopped and stared at Uncle, but he strode on with his boards and tool-box as if nothing had happened.

Then Milly-Molly-Mandy began

jumping up and down in a great hurry and said, "What's a Milly-Molly-Mandy nest, Uncle? What's it like, Uncle? Where is it, Uncle? DO-O tell me!"

"Well," said Uncle, "you ought to know what a Milly-Molly-Mandy nest is, being a Milly-Molly-Mandy yourself. It's up in the big old oak-tree at the bottom of the meadow."

So Milly-Molly-Mandy tore off to the big old oak-tree at the bottom of the meadow, but she couldn't see any sort of a nest there, only Uncle's ladder leaning against the tree.

Uncle put the boards and tool-box carefully down on the ground, then he settled the ladder against the big old oak-tree, then he picked up Milly-Molly-Mandy and carried her up the ladder and sat her on a nice safe branch.

And then Milly-Molly-Mandy saw

there was a big hollow in the big old oak-tree (which was a very big old oak-tree indeed). And it was such a big hollow that Uncle could get right inside it himself and leave quite a lot of room over.

"Now, Milly-Molly-Mandy," said Uncle, "you can perch on that branch and chirp a bit while I put your nest in order."

Then Uncle went down the ladder and brought up some of the boards and the tool-box, which he hung by its handle on a sticking-out branch. And Milly-Molly-Mandy watched while Uncle measured off boards and sawed them and fitted them and hammered nails into them, until he had made a beautiful flat floor in the hollow in the big old oak-tree, so that it looked like the nicest little fairy-tale room you ever saw!

Then he hoisted Milly-Molly-Mandy off the branch, where she had been chirping with excitement like the biggest sparrow you ever saw (only that you never saw a sparrow in a pink-and-white striped cotton frock), and heaved her up into the hollow.

And Milly-Molly-Mandy stood on the beautiful flat floor and touched the funny brown walls of the big old oak-tree's inside, and looked out of the opening on to the grass down below, and thought a Milly-Molly-Mandy nest was the very nicest and excitingest place to be in the whole wide world!

Just then whom should she see wandering along the road at the end of the meadow but little-friend-Susan!

"Susan!" called Milly-Molly-Mandy as loud as ever she could, waving her arms as hard as ever she could. And little-friend-Susan peeped over the hedge.

At first she didn't see Milly-Molly-Mandy up in her nest, and then she did, and she jumped up and down and waved; and Milly-Molly-Mandy beckoned, and little-friend-Susan ran to the meadow-gate and couldn't get it open because she was in such a hurry, and tried to get through and couldn't because she was too big, and began to climb over and couldn't because it was rather high. So at last she squeezed round the side of the gate-post through a little gap in the hedge and came racing across the meadow to the big old oak-tree, and Uncle helped her up.

And then Milly-Molly-Mandy and little-friend-Susan sat and hugged themselves together, up in the Milly-Molly-Mandy nest.

Just then Father came by the big old oak-tree, and when he saw what was going on he went and got a rope and threw up one end to Milly-Molly-Mandy. And then Father tied an empty wooden box to the other end, and Milly-Molly-Mandy pulled it up and untied it and set it in the middle of the floor like a little table.

Then Mother, who had been watching from the gate of the nice white cottage with the thatched roof, came and tied an old rug to the end of the rope, and little-friend-Susan pulled it up and spread it on the floor like a carpet.

Then Grandpa came along, and he tied some fine ripe plums in a basket to the end of the rope, and Milly-Molly-Mandy pulled them up and set them on the little table.

Then Grandma came across the meadow bringing some old cushions, and she tied them to the end of the rope, and little-friend-Susan pulled them up and arranged them on the carpet.

Then Aunty came along, and she tied a little flower vase on the end of the rope, and Milly-Molly-Mandy pulled it up and set it in the middle of the table. And now the Milly-Molly-Mandy nest was properly furnished, and Milly-Molly-Mandy was in such a hurry to get Billy Blunt to come to see it that she could hardly get down from it quickly enough.

Mother said, "You may ask little-friend-Susan and Billy Blunt to tea up there if you like, Milly-Molly-Mandy."

So Milly-Molly-Mandy and little-friend-Susan ran off straight away, hoppity-skip

to the Moggses' cottage (for little-friend-Susan to ask Mrs Moggs's permission), and to the village to Mr Blunt's corn-shop (to ask Billy Blunt), while Uncle fixed steps up the big old oak-tree, so that they could climb easily to the nest.

And at five o'clock that very afternoon Milly-Molly-Mandy and little-friend-Susan and Billy Blunt were sitting drinking milk from three little mugs and eating slices of bread-and-jam and gingerbread from three little plates, and feeling just as excited and comfortable and happy as ever they could be, up in the Milly-Molly-Mandy nest!

Milly-Molly-Mandy
Goes for a Picnic

Once upon a time Milly-Molly-Mandy was going for a picnic.

It was a real, proper picnic. Father and Mother and Uncle and Aunty were all going too, and little-friend-Susan and Billy Blunt (because it wouldn't seem quite a real, proper picnic without little-friend-Susan and Billy Blunt).

They were going to take the red bus from the cross-roads to a specially nice picnic place, where Milly-Molly-Mandy hadn't ever been before because it was quite a long way off. (The nicest places often do seem to be quite a long way off, somehow.)

Grandpa and Grandma weren't going. They said they would rather stay at home in the nice white cottage with the thatched roof, and keep house and milk the cows if the picnickers weren't back in time.

It was a quiet, misty sort of morning, which looked as if it meant to turn out a fine hot day, as Father and Mother and Uncle and Aunty and Milly-Molly-Mandy (and Toby the dog) set off down the road to the village, carrying the picnic things.

When they came to the Moggses' cottage little-friend-Susan (in a clean cotton frock) was ready and waiting for them at the gate.

And when they came to Mr Blunt's corn-shop Billy Blunt (in a new khaki shirt with pockets) was ready and waiting for them by the side-door.

And when they came to the cross-roads

Milly-Molly-Mandy was going for a picnic

the red bus was already at the bus-stop. And as, of course, it wouldn't wait long for them, they all had to run like anything. But they just caught it, and climbed inside.

Father took the tickets.

Let's see: Father and Mother and Uncle and Aunty – that's four grown-up tickets. And little-friend-Susan and Billy Blunt and Milly-Molly-Mandy – that's three half-tickets. (Father had asked the bus-conductor as they got on, "Do you mind the dog?" And the bus-conductor didn't, so Toby rode under the seat for nothing.)

Milly-Molly-Mandy said to little-friend-Susan and Billy Blunt as the bus went rattling along: "You haven't been to this place before, have you?" (hoping they hadn't).

Billy Blunt said: "Once. But I don't remember it. I was young then."

Little-friend-Susan said: "No. But my

father and mother went a long time ago, and they say it's a nice place, and there's a wishing-well there, and you can drop a pin in and wish."

Billy Blunt said: "Don't believe in wishing-wells. Can't make the things come true. Not if they aren't really."

And Milly-Molly-Mandy said: "Oh, neither do I. But it's fun to pretend!"

And little-friend-Susan thought so too.

When they came to the next village (where the bus turned round ready to go back again) they all had to get out and walk. Father and Mother and Uncle and Aunty walked in two's, and Milly-Molly-Mandy and little-friend-Susan and Billy Blunt walked all in a bunch. And Toby the dog ran here and there, snorting into holes and getting his nose muddy. (He did enjoy it!)

The sun shone hot now, and they began to get quite thirsty. But Mother said: "We're nearly there, and then you can have a nice drink at the well!" And Aunty gave them some fruit-sweets wrapped in coloured papers.

Milly-Molly-Mandy and little-friend-Susan put their sweet wrappers into their baskets, and Billy Blunt put his into one of his shirt pockets, to throw away when they got home.

Father said: "Well, anyone can see you've been properly brought up!"

He wished every one who used that path did the same. He kept poking other people's bits of sweet-paper and orange-peel into the hedge with his stick as he went along, because they made the path look so nasty.

Mother said: "I think a place ought to look nicer because we've been there, not nastier!"

And Milly-Molly-Mandy and little-friend-Susan thought the same. Billy Blunt found a stick, and helped to poke the litter away too.

At last they came to the specially nice

picnic place. And it really was almost like a fairy glen, with daisies and buttercups, and grassy slopes, and trees to climb, and a little stream running through the middle.

But – other people must have been there for picnics too, for – would you believe it? – they had left paper bags and egg-shells and litter everywhere. (And it almost spoiled everywhere, I can tell you.)

"Oh dear!" said Father and Mother and Uncle and Aunty, looking all about.

"Where's the wishing-well?" asked Milly-Molly-Mandy and little-friend-Susan and Billy Blunt, looking all about too.

Father led the way to where some big, old trees were stooping round as if trying to hide something. And in behind them Milly-Molly-Mandy and little-friend-Susan and Billy Blunt saw a deep round hole in a wet rock which was simply covered over with beautiful green ferns and moss. And water, sparkling like crystal and cold as ice, was dripping down into it over the mossy rocks at the back.

It really did look just like a wishing-well!

Milly-Molly-Mandy and little-friend-Susan and Billy Blunt leaned over to see if they could see any pins lying at the bottom.

But – other people must have been there too, and – would you believe it? – they had thrown in old tins and ice-cream cartons and litter, and there it was all lying under the water that was clear as crystal and cold as ice.

"Oh, *dear*!" said Milly-Molly-Mandy and little-friend-Susan and Billy Blunt. "Oh, dear; oh, dear!"

For you couldn't think of dropping a pin in and wishing there. You couldn't even have a drink.

Then Father said: "Mates, there's a spot of work to be done around here. We'd better get busy."

And he fished up some rusty tins out of the well with his stick.

Then Billy Blunt fished out some wet papers and cartons with his stick. And Milly-Molly-Mandy   and   little-friend-

Susan picked up bits of silver-paper and bus-tickets scattered about. And Father buried it all down a hole under a rock, where it couldn't be seen.

The well didn't look clear now, but Father said it would soon settle and be crystal clear again, as a wishing-well should be. So they thought they had better wait before making their wishes.

Meantime Mother and Aunty had chosen the best spot for the picnic, so Milly-Molly-Mandy and little-friend-Susan and Billy Blunt got busy collecting all the scraps of paper lying about, and Uncle put a match to them. (He took good care to do it where nothing else could catch fire or hurt the growing things, because, of course, when you have roots like trees and plants you can't move out of the way when you're getting hurt!) Billy Blunt collected bits of broken glass too, lest Toby the dog should cut his paws, and Father buried it safely.

By then it was time for the picnic, so they all washed their hands in the little stream running through the middle, and sat down to enjoy themselves.

They had hard-boiled eggs, and brown bread-and-butter, and cheese, and tomatoes, and buns and a big jam-tart. And to drink there was hot tea from a Thermos for the grown-ups, and cold milk for the young ones. And they were all so thirsty they drank up every drop. (Toby the dog drank all he wanted from the little stream.)

When every one had quite done they packed everything tidily away in their baskets to take home with them, all their empty bottles and wrapping-papers and string.

And then Father gave a great sigh of satisfaction, and lay back in the sunshine and put his hat over his face. And Mother sat in the shade and took up her knitting. And Uncle pulled out his newspaper with the cross-word puzzle. And Aunty opened her nice new lady's magazine.

But Milly-Molly-Mandy and little-friend-Susan and Billy Blunt (and Toby the dog) all wanted to be up and doing. So they ran about, paddling in the little stream and climbing the trees and playing hide-and-seek. And wherever they went they tidied up until there wasn't a bit of litter to be seen.

"Well!" said Milly-Molly-Mandy, looking about when it was almost time to go. "This picnic place looks ever so much nicer now *we've* visited it! I should think the next people would be pleased."

"I wish," said little-friend-Susan, "everybody would leave nice places nice when they visit them."

That made Billy Blunt remember something. And he said:

"We never made our wishes at the wishing-well."

So they all three rushed over to the wishing-well. And there it was, clear as crystal and cold as ice right down to the bottom, as a wishing-well should be. Mother gave them a cup, and they all drank, and filled up their bottle.

"Dropping just a pin in won't spoil it

now, will it?" said Milly-Molly-Mandy.

"We can't make a proper wish without a pin," said little-friend-Susan.

"Won't make any difference anyhow," said Billy Blunt.

But he looked a bit disappointed, all the same, when Mother could find only two pins, which she gave to Milly-Molly-Mandy and little-friend-Susan. But then Father found one under his coat lapel, and handed it to Billy Blunt. And Billy Blunt looked quite pleased as he took it!

So they each dropped a pin into the wishing-well, and solemnly wished.

They couldn't tell their wishes out loud, because that might have spoiled the magic! But I *think* they all wished the same wish. And as Father said, if enough people wish a wish, and it's a *good* wish, it's quite likely to come to pass.

So let's hope that Milly-Molly-Mandy's
and little-friend-Susan's and Billy Blunt's
wishes all come true!

Milly-Molly-Mandy
On Bank Holiday

Once upon a time, one fine day, Milly-Molly-Mandy couldn't think what to do with herself.

It felt as if something specially nice should be done, as it was a Bank Holiday. But Father and Mother and Grandpa and Grandma and Uncle and Aunty all said they were busy, and everywhere would be so crowded today, and they preferred to stay at home.

"Why not go and play with little-friend-Susan?" said Mother, getting out jam-pots ready for jam-making.

"Get yourself some sweets, if the shop's open," said Father, feeling in his trousers' pocket.

So Milly-Molly-Mandy called to Toby the dog and wandered down the road with the hedges each side, to the Moggses' cottage.

Little-friend-Susan was outside, minding her baby sister.

They both had clean frocks and their hats on.

"Hullo, Milly-Molly-Mandy!" said little-friend Susan. "It's Bank Holiday today. Father's going to take us all out on the red bus. I wish you were coming too!"

So did Milly-Molly-

Mandy. But as she wasn't she called to Toby the dog and wandered on down to the village.

Miss Muggins's shop had its blind half-down over the toys and sweets in the window. But Milly-Molly-Mandy tried the handle, just in case, and Miss Muggins's Jilly peeped through the collarettes and gloves hanging across the glass of the door.

When she saw who was there Miss Muggins's Jilly stooped and said through the letter-box slit:

"We aren't open today, Milly-Molly-Mandy. It's Bank Holiday. My aunty's taking me to my granny's, by the red bus."

(Toby the dog was so surprised at a voice coming from the letter-box that he barked and barked!)

But next moment the door was unlocked, and Miss Muggins's Jilly (in her best white hat) stepped outside, followed by

Miss Muggins herself (in her best black).

As she locked the door behind her and put the key in her bag Miss Muggins said:

"Good morning, Milly-Molly-Mandy. Now we mustn't delay, or we shall miss the bus."

And Milly-Molly-Mandy, holding Toby the dog, watched them go hurrying down to the cross-roads, where several people were standing waiting.

The red bus arrived just as Mr Moggs, carrying the baby, and Mrs Moggs, with little-friend-Susan, came running and waving by the short-cut across the fields, only *just* in time. Everybody scrambled aboard; the bus gave a "ping!" and off they all went, away into the distance.

And you wouldn't believe how empty the village felt!

There was only Mr Smale the grocer (in his shirtsleeves) reading a newspaper

"Hullo!" he said, grinning

at his doorway, and Milly-Molly-Mandy standing with Toby the dog, wondering what to do next.

There didn't seem to be anything.

Then, round the corner by the forge, who should come along but Billy Blunt, carrying an old rusty tea-tray under his arm!

"Hullo!" he said, grinning.

"Hullo!" said Milly-Molly-Mandy, rather dolefully. "It's Bank Holiday today."

"I know," said Billy Blunt. "And I mean to have one. You can come along if you want."

"Where to?" asked Milly-Molly-Mandy. "What are you going to do? What's that thing?"

"It's a tea-tray," said Billy Blunt. "I found it on Mr Rudge's junk-heap. I shall put it back when I've done. Come on if you're coming."

So, feeling very curious, Milly-Molly-Mandy and Toby the dog followed him.

They walked to the cross-roads, then up the steep hilly road beyond. Presently they climbed a low fence and through a lot of brambles and things, till they came out on a high meadow looking down on the village. "Here's the place," said Billy Blunt.

And he solemnly placed his tray on the ground and sat on it. And with a few shoves and pushes he went sliding down over the grass, faster and faster down the bank, leaving Milly-Molly-Mandy and Toby the dog shouting and barking behind him, till at last he came to a stop by the hedge at the bottom of the meadow.

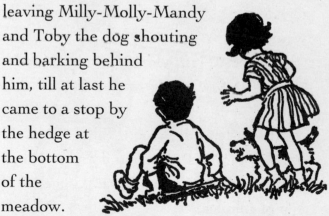

"How's that?" he said triumphantly, as he climbed panting back to the top again, dragging the tray. "Want a go? You have to mind out for the nettles by the hedge . . ."

So Milly-Molly-Mandy sat on the tray, and Billy Blunt gave her a good shove. And off she went down the bank, with the wind in her hair and Toby the dog racing alongside, till she spilled over in the long grass just short of the nettles.

Then Billy Blunt took several more turns till he was quite out of breath, and Milly-Molly-Mandy had another go.

They only stopped at last because it began to feel like dinner-time. They were very hungry and very warm (and rather grubby too!).

"Well!" said Milly-Molly-Mandy, as they started homeward, "this is a proper Bank Holiday, isn't it?"

"Well," said Billy Blunt, "I think Bank Holidays are meant so that people in banks can stop counting up their money. It's not this sort of bank really, you know."

"This is the sort of Bank Holiday I like best, anyhow," said Milly-Molly-Mandy.

Milly-Molly-Mandy
Finds a Train

Once upon a time Milly-Molly-Mandy was playing with Billy Blunt down by the little brook (which, you know, ran through the fields at the back of the nice white cottage with the thatched roof where Milly-Molly-Mandy lived).

They had got their shoes and socks off, and were paddling about in the water, and poking about among the stones and moss, and enjoying themselves very much. Only it was so interesting just about where their feet were that they might have missed seeing something else interesting, a little farther off, if a woodpecker hadn't suddenly started pecking in an old tree near by, and made Billy Blunt look up.

He didn't see the woodpecker, but he did see the something else.

"I say – what's that, there?" said Billy Blunt, standing up and staring.

"What's what, where?" said Milly-Molly-Mandy, standing up and staring too.

"There," said Billy Blunt, pointing.

And Milly-Molly-Mandy looked there. And she saw, in the meadow on the farther side of the brook, what looked like a railway train. Only there was no railway near the meadow.

"It looks like a train," said Milly-Molly-Mandy.

"Um-m," said Billy Blunt.

"But how did it get there?" said Milly-Molly-Mandy.

"Must have been pulled there," said
Billy Blunt.

"But what for? Who put it there? When
did it come?" said Milly-Molly-Mandy.

Billy Blunt didn't answer. He splashed
back to get his boots and socks, and he
splashed across the brook with them, and
sat on the grass on the other side, and began
to dab his feet with his handkerchief. So

Milly-Molly-Mandy splashed across with her shoes and began to put them on too. And with her toes scrunched up in the shoes (because they were still damp and wouldn't straighten out at first) she ran and hopped after Billy Blunt, up the little bank and across the grass to the train.

They walked all round it, staring hard. It hadn't got an engine, or a guard's van. It was just a railway carriage, and it stood with its big iron wheels in the grass, looking odd and out-of-place among the daisies and buttercups.

"It's like a funny sort of house," said Milly-Molly-Mandy, climbing up to peep in the windows. "I wish we could play in it. Look – that could be the kitchen, and that's the sitting-room, and that's the bedroom. I wish we could get in!"

It had several doors either side, each with a big 3 painted on. Billy Blunt tried the handles in turn. They all seemed to be locked. But the last one wasn't! It opened heavily, and they could get into one compartment.

"It's old," said Billy Blunt, looking about. "I expect they've thrown it away."

"What a waste!" said Milly-Molly-Mandy. "Well, it's ours now. We found it. We can live in it, and go on journeys!"

It was very exciting. They shut the door and they opened the windows. And then they sat down on the two wooden seats, and pretended they were going away for a holiday. When they stood up, or walked to the windows to look out, it was difficult to do it steadily, because the train rushed along so fast! Once it let out a great long whistle, so that Milly-Molly-Mandy jumped; and Billy Blunt grinned and did it again.

"We are just going through a station," he explained.

The next moment Milly-Molly-Mandy nearly fell over and knocked Billy Blunt.

"We've stopped suddenly – the signal must be up," she explained. So they each hung out of a window to look. "Now it's down and we're going on again," said Milly-Molly-Mandy.

"We're going into a tunnel now," said Billy Blunt, pulling up his window by the strap. So Milly-Molly-Mandy pulled up hers – to keep the smoke out!

When the train stopped at last they got out, and everything looked quite different all round. They were by the sea, and the train was a house. One of the seats was a table, and they laid Billy Blunt's damp handkerchief on it as a tablecloth, and put a rusty tin filled with buttercups in the middle.

But after a while Billy Blunt began to feel hungry, and then, of course, they knew it must be time to think of going home. So

They walked all round it, staring hard

at last they shut the door of their wonderful train-house, and planned to meet there again as early as possible the next day.

And then they jumped back over the brook, and Billy Blunt went one way across the field, to his home by the corn-shop; and Milly-Molly-Mandy went the other way across the field, to the nice white cottage with the thatched roof, where she found Father and Mother and Grandpa and Grandma and Uncle and Aunty just ready to sit down to table.

The next day Milly-Molly-Mandy hurried to get all her jobs done – helping to wash up the breakfast things, and make the beds, and do the dusting. And as soon as she was free to play she ran straight out and down to the brook.

Billy Blunt was just coming across the field from the village, so she waited for him, and together they crossed over the brook, planning where they would go for their travels today.

"There it is!" said Milly-Molly-Mandy, almost as if she had expected the train to have run away in the night.

And then she stopped. And Billy Blunt stopped too.

There was a man with a cap on, sitting on the roof of the train, fixing up a sort of chimney. And there was a woman with an apron on, sweeping dust out of one of the doorways. And there was a baby in a shabby old pram near by, squealing. And there was a little dog, guarding a hand-cart piled with boxes and bundles, who barked when he saw Milly-Molly-Mandy and Billy Blunt.

"They've got our train!" said Milly-Molly-Mandy, staring.

"'Spect it's their train, really," said Billy Blunt.

Milly-Molly-Mandy edged a little nearer and spoke to the little dog, who got under the cart and barked again (but he wagged his tail at the same time). The woman in the apron looked up and saw them.

Milly-Molly-Mandy said, "Good morning. Is this your train?"

"Yes, it is," said the woman, knocking dust out of the broom.

"Are you going to live in it?" asked Milly-Molly-Mandy.

"Yes, we are," said the woman. "Bought and paid for it, we did, and got it towed here, and it's going to be our home now."

"Is this your baby?" asked Billy Blunt, jiggling the

pram gently. The baby stopped crying and stared up at him. "What's its name?"

The woman smiled then. "His name is Thomas Thomas, like his father's," she said. "So it don't matter whether you call either of 'em by surname or given-name, it's all one."

Just then the man on the roof dropped his hammer down into the grass, and called out, "Here, mate, just chuck that up, will you?"

So Billy Blunt threw the hammer up, and the man caught it and went on fixing the chimney, while Billy Blunt watched and handed up other things as they were wanted. And the man told him that this end of the carriage was going to be the kitchen (just as Milly-Molly-Mandy had planned!), and the wall between it and the next compartment was to be taken away so as to make it bigger. The other end was the bedroom, with the long seats for beds.

Milly-Molly-Mandy stayed jiggling the pram to keep the baby quiet, and making friends with the little dog. And the woman told her she had got some stuff for window-curtains in the hand-cart there; and that they planned to make a bit of a garden round, to grow potatoes and cabbages in, so the house would soon look more proper. She said her husband was a tinker, and he hoped to get work mending pots and kettles in the villages near, instead of tramping about the country looking for it, as they had been doing.

She asked Milly-Molly-Mandy if she didn't think the baby would have quite a nice home, after a bit? And Milly-Molly-Mandy said she DID!

Presently the woman brought out from the hand-cart a frying-pan, and a newspaper parcel of sausages, and a kettle (which Milly-Molly-Mandy filled for her at the brook). So then Milly-Molly-Mandy and Billy Blunt knew it was time to be going.

They said goodbye to the man and woman, and stroked the little dog. (The baby was asleep.) And as they were crossing back over the brook the man called after them:

"If you've got any pots, pans, and kettles to mend, you know where to come to find Thomas Tinker!"

So after that Milly-Molly-Mandy and Billy Blunt were always on the look-out for anyone who had a saucepan, frying-pan, or kettle which leaked or had a loose handle, and offered at once to take it to Thomas Tinker's to be mended. And people were very pleased, because Thomas Tinker mended small things quicker than Mr Rudge the blacksmith did, not being so busy making horse-shoes and mending ploughs and big things. Thomas Tinker and his wife were very grateful to Milly-Molly-Mandy and Billy Blunt.

But as Milly-Molly-Mandy said, "If we can get them plenty of work then they can go on living here. And if we can't have that train for ourselves I like next best for Mr Tinker and Mrs Tinker and Baby Tinker to have it – don't you, Billy?"

And Billy Blunt did.

Joyce Lankester Brisley

MILLY-MOLLY-MANDY'S Autumn

*Autumn is a very
busy time for
Milly-Molly-Mandy*

It's a blustery autumn and Milly-Molly-Mandy
has lots to do! Join her on Guy Fawkes Night,
discover the secret plant that is growing in
her garden and attend a wedding that
ends with a bang!

Joyce Lankester Brisley

MILLY-MOLLY-MANDY'S Friends

*"Let's both dress up and be
ladies," said Milly-Molly-Mandy.
"Ooh, yes, let's,"
said little-friend-Susan.*

Milly-Molly-Mandy has lots of friends, but her favourite
companions are little-friend-Susan and Billy Blunt.
Join them on five of their exciting adventures as they
run races, pay visits, rescue rabbits, play tricks on one
another and deal with a gang of naughty boys!

MILLY-MOLLY-MANDY'S
Things to Make and Do

Based on the stories by
JOYCE LANKESTER BRISLEY

Whether she's baking a cake, planting a
miniature garden or having a dolls' tea-party,
Milly-Molly-Mandy is always having fun.
Packed with teatime treats, crafty fun and big ideas
to brighten up a gloomy day, this is the perfect
book for long holidays, rainy days and
adventures in your own back garden!

With easy-to-follow instructions for lots of
wonderful activities, including:

- ❖ Baking blackberry
  crumble
- ❖ Sewing patchwork
- ❖ Knitting a scarf

- ❖ Planting sunflowers
- ❖ Identifying leaves
- ❖ Building a fort
- ❖ Making a bird feeder

And much, much more!

Joyce Lankester Brisley

MILLY-MOLLY-MANDY'S Spring

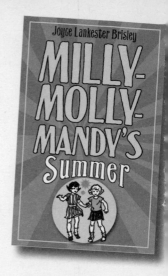

Joyce Lankester Brisley

MILLY-MOLLY-MANDY'S Summer

Collect them all!

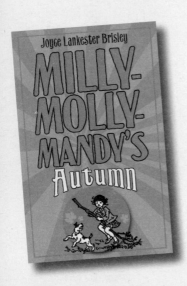

Joyce Lankester Brisley

MILLY-MOLLY-MANDY'S Autumn

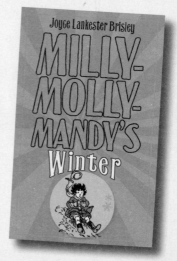

Joyce Lankester Brisley

MILLY-MOLLY-MANDY'S Winter

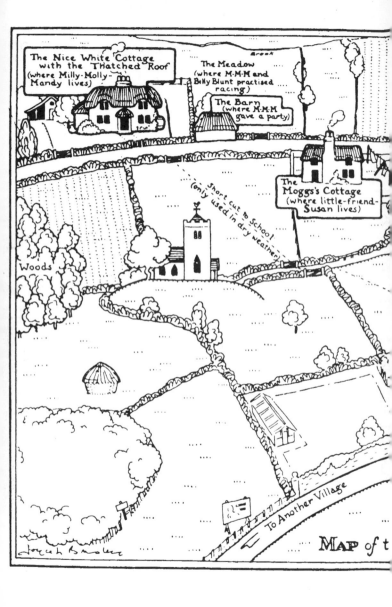